MIDNIGHT VISIT
AT MOLLY'S HOUSE

*Written and illustrated
by Jirina Marton*

Annick Press, Toronto, M2M 1H9

Annick Press gratefully acknowledges the support of The
Canada Council and the Ontario Arts Council

CANADIAN CATALOGUING in PUBLICATION DATA

Marton, Jirina.
  Midnight visit at Molly's house

ISBN 0-920303-99-4 (bound). – ISBN 0-920303-98-6 (pbk.)

I. Title

PS8576.A774M53 1988   jC813'.54   C87-095283-8
PZ7.M373Mi   1988

Annick Press books are distributed in Canada and the USA
by:
Firefly Books Ltd.,
3520 Pharmacy Ave., Unit 1c
Scarborough, Ontario   M1W 2T8

Printed and bound in Canada

For Michelle Anna

Once upon a time there was a town, and above that town, night after night, shone the Moon. Every evening, it rose on one side of the town, and every morning, it went down on the other. One night, when it was mid-way over the town, something crossed its mind. "I shine down on this town every night," said the Moon, "but I don't know what the town looks like from up close. How would it be if I slipped down a little lower and saw for myself?"

It was a beautiful, balmy summer night, long past midnight. The town was quiet and everyone was sound asleep. The Moon slid down from its place high above and began to explore the town. First it went along the broad avenues and boulevards, then along the narrower streets and laneways, until at last it came to the smallest street of all. At the very end of this tiny street, there was a garden with a pink house. And in that pink house lived a father and a mother and their little girl, Molly.

The Moon loved the garden. It was magnificent, with trees and shrubs and flowers and little white pathways winding this way and that. There even was a pond. It floated up and down, until finally one of the little white pathways led it right up to the pink house.

"I'll take a look through the window," said the Moon. "After all, I've never seen the inside of a house before." And so it peeped through the open window of Molly's bedroom. Molly was already sound asleep, so she didn't see the inquisitive Moon looking in.

At first the Moon just peered very cautiously over the window-sill. The house was quiet. Nothing moved. The Moon floated over the sill and into the room. What a lot of things there were to see! "If only I had more time," thought the Moon, "I'd go for a ride on the tricycle, or read Molly's books, or play with the toy cars, or perhaps I'd even try to draw something." But time was short and it wanted to explore the whole house, so it hurried on.

It looked in the door opposite Molly's room. It was a bathroom. What a lot of things there were to see! "If only I had more time," thought the Moon, "I could try a nice warm bath with the boat, the lamb and the big fish." But time was short and it wanted to explore the whole house, so it hurried on.

It looked into another room. It was the bedroom where Molly's Mommy and Daddy slept. What a lot of things there were to see. A sweater and tie on a chair, slippers under the bed, a big mirror on a wall. "If only I had more time," thought the Moon, "I'd sleep like a baby on such a nice bed." But time was short and it wanted to explore the whole house, so it hurried on.

It went down the stairs and into the living room. What a lot of things there were to see. A painting, a fireplace and flowers in a vase. "If only I had more time," thought the Moon, "I'd sit down in the easy chair and just take it easy." But time was short and it wanted to explore the whole house, so it hurried on.

The last door led to the kitchen. There was still a hint of delicious smells. The table was set for three. "If only I had more time," thought the Moon, "I'd wait till morning and have breakfast with everyone." The Moon looked at the kitchen clock and was startled to see how late it was. Now it had to hurry to make up for lost time. And so the Moon went back up into the sky.

The Moon smiled one last time at the pink house in
the small town, then slowly sank behind the horizon,
taking the darkness with it. The stars faded. Then the
sky turned pink and suddenly, out of that pink, up
popped the sun and announced a bright, new day.

Molly woke up. She'd had a dream about the Moon. At least she thought she had. Or had the Moon really come down for a visit? She giggled. Then she said good morning to the sun, yawned and stretched, and put her dream about the Moon right out of her mind.